Hamlet 2.
StuART Little
IVy + Bean

First edition
2 4 6 8 10 9 7 5 3 1

Library of Congress Cataloging-in-Publication Data
Perrault, Charles, 1628–1703.
[Cendrillon. English]
Cinderella : a fairy tale / by Charles Perrault ; illustrated by
Edith Baudrand. — 1st ed.
p.   cm. — (The little pebbles)
Summary: With the help of her fairy godmother, a kitchen maid
mistreated by her stepmother and stepsisters attends the palace ball
where she meets the prince of her dreams.
ISBN 0-7892-0512-2
[1. Fairy tales. 2. Folklore–France.] I. Baudrand, Edith, ill.
II. Title. III. Series.
PZ7.P426Ci   1999
398.2'0944'02–dc21   98-35942
[E]

Cinderella

A Fairy Tale by Charles Perrault
Illustrated by Édith Baudrand

· Abbeville Kids ·

A Division of Abbeville Publishing Group

New York · London · Paris

Once upon a time there was a gentleman. After the death of his first wife, he married again. His new wife was proud and haughty, as were her two daughters. His own daughter, however, was exceptionally gentle and kind.

All too soon after the wedding, the stepmother revealed her true nature. She couldn't stand the kindness of her husband's daughter. Nor could her two daughters.

The stepmother made the poor girl do all the housework and sent her to sleep on a straw mattress in the attic. When she finished her work, she would sit in a corner next to the fireplace, among the ashes and cinders. So her stepsisters, to make fun of her, called her Cinderella. But their laughter meant nothing, for Cinderella's beauty and good nature shone through even her ragged clothing.

One day, the son of the king announced a grand ball. Many young ladies were invited, including the two stepsisters. The house buzzed with their excitement—they could speak of nothing else!

Anyone but Cinderella would have messed up their hair after hearing that, but Cinderella did their hair perfectly.

The night of the ball finally arrived, and the two sisters left in the highest spirits. When they were gone, Cinderella began to cry.

"You would like to go to the ball, wouldn't you?" asked a voice.

With those words, her godmother, who was a fairy, appeared before her.

"Oh, yes!" sighed Cinderella through her tears.

"Well then, you will go! I promise. Run to the garden and bring me a pumpkin."

Cinderella picked the most beautiful pumpkin that she could find. Her fairy godmother hollowed it out and struck it with her wand: the pumpkin immediately became a beautiful coach made entirely of gold.

"Now, Cinderella, open the mousetrap," asked the godmother.

Cinderella obeyed and, with a wave of the wand, each mouse that scurried out was transformed into a dappled gray horse. And so the carriage had a magnificent team of horses to pull it.

Then, with two more waves of the wand, the fairy godmother transformed a rat into a stout coach driver with a superb mustache, and six lizards into footmen dressed in bright colors.

"There, you have what you need to go to the ball, Cinderella! Are you pleased?" asked her godmother.

"Oh, yes. . . . But I can't go in my ugly clothes!"

So her godmother touched her with her wand, and her rags were transformed into a gold and silver gown, embroidered with precious gems, and a pair of dazzling glass slippers.

But she warned Cinderella, "Make sure you leave the ball before midnight! At midnight, everything will return to what it was before."

"I will!" said Cinderella, and off she went.

When she reached the castle, the king's son hurried to welcome her. He had been told that a great but unknown princess had just arrived.

He took her by the hand and brought her to the ballroom. The room fell silent; everyone stopped dancing, and the violins stopped playing; all eyes were on the stranger who had just entered. A murmur filled the room. "Oh! How beautiful. . . . How beautiful she is!" could be heard everywhere.

The king's son asked her to dance. She was so graceful and so light that she was admired even more. He did not leave her side for the entire evening. He spoke to her and danced with her all night.

Cinderella, charmed by his words, forgot everything. She even forgot what her godmother had told her. Only when she heard the first stroke of midnight did she remember. She leapt up and rushed out at once.

Cinderella reached home completely out of breath, without a coach or footman, and wearing her usual ugly clothes. When her two sisters returned from the ball, they told her:

"Tonight a magnificent princess came to the ball. At midnight, she ran out so quickly that she lost one of her small glass slippers. The king's son picked it up and gazed at it for the rest of the night!"

"He must be in love with this princess."

What the two sisters said was the truth, for a few days later, the son of the king announced that he would marry the woman whose foot fit the slipper.

First, all the ladies of the court tried it on, but in vain. Then it was sent throughout the kingdom. The two sisters did everything they could to fit a foot into the slipper. They did not succeed.

"Let's see if it fits me!" Cinderella said suddenly.

The sisters began to laugh and tease her.

But the gentleman who brought the slipper thought Cinderella was very beautiful.

"I have been instructed to have all the young women of the land try on the slipper. "Miss," he said to Cinderella, "please sit down and see if it fits you."

Cinderella sat down, and without any difficulty put the slipper on her foot.

The two sisters were stunned—and even more so when Cinderella took the other slipper out of her pocket.

On top of everything, the fairy godmother returned, and, with a stroke of her wand, transformed Cinderella's clothing.

"Oh, the princess from the ball!" the two sisters cried out. "Forgive us, forgive us for all the bad things we did to you!" And they threw themselves at her feet. Cinderella forgave them. Then, she went to meet the king's son, who found her even more beautiful than he remembered. They were married a few days later.

And Cinderella, as good as she was beautiful, invited her two sisters to live in the castle, and married them off to two of the lords at the court.

Look carefully at these pictures from the story. They're all mixed up. Can you put them back in the right order?

a

b

c

d

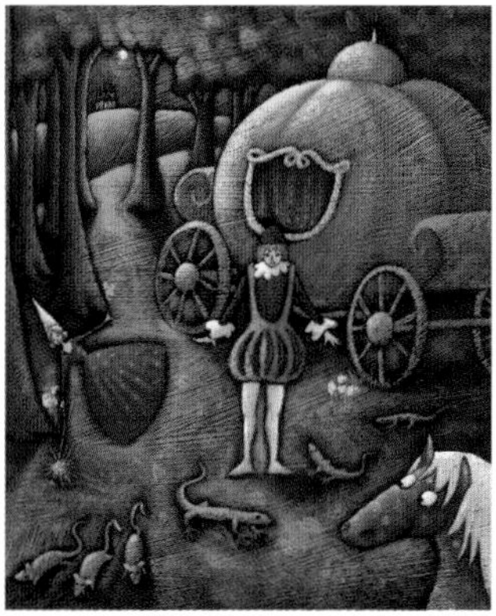

e

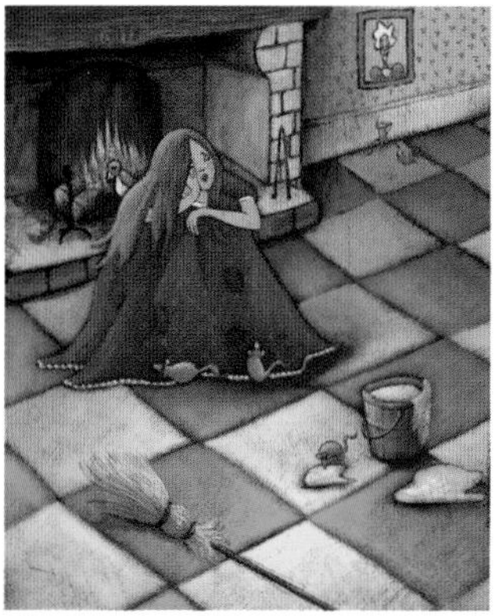

f

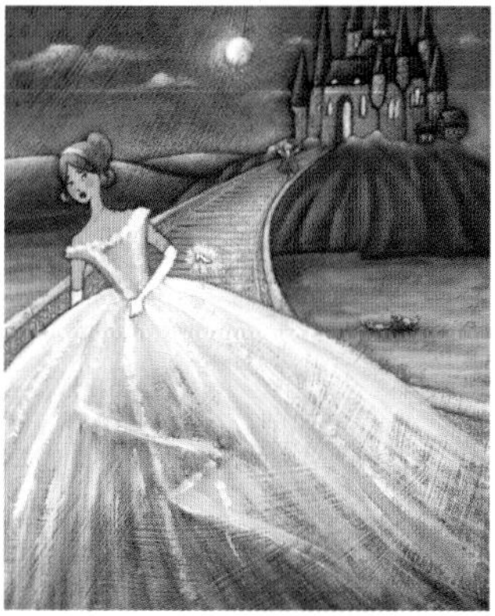

g

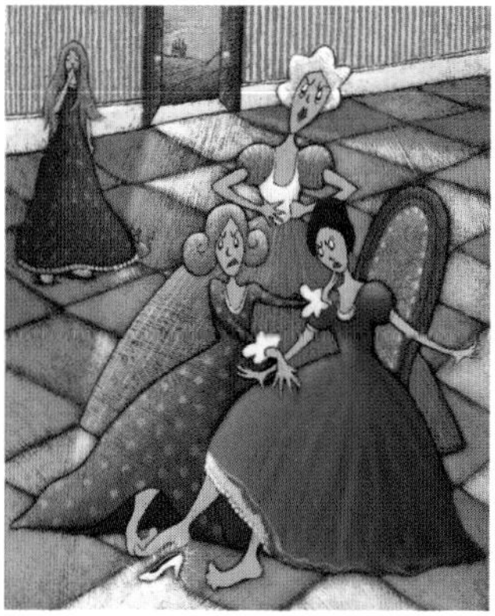

h

Correct order: c, d, f, e, b, g, h, a